The Magic Music Box

By Katie Dale

Illustrated by Giovana Medeiros

Chapter 1

Bella loved to dance. Everywhere she went, she twirled and leaped and skipped.

She waltzed in the woods. She jived past the jewellers. She pirouetted in the park. She did salsa in the supermarket. But Bella's favourite dance of all was ballet.

One day, a new ballet school opened in town. “Can I join, Mum?” she begged. “Please?”

The Magic Music Box

T
a

Maverick
Early Readers

'The Magic Music Box'
An original concept by Katie Dale

Illustrated by Giovana Medeiros

Published by MAVERICK ARTS PUBLISHING LTD

Studio 3A, City Business Centre, 6 Brighton Road,

Horsham, West Sussex, RH13 5BB

+44 (0)1403 256941

A CIP catalogue record for this book is available at the British Library.

ISBN 978-1-84886-417-7

www.maverickbooks.co.uk

This book is rated as: Gold Band (Guided Reading)

Ballet
SCHOOL

“I'm sorry, Bella,” said her mum. “Ballet's too expensive. You'd need ballet shoes and a leotard and a tutu.”

Bella saved up all her pocket money, and every week she did the cha-cha-cha to the charity shop. Finally, she found a second-hand leotard, tutu, and ballet slippers.

“They're my size!” Bella cried happily, handing over her pocket money.

“I've got everything I need, Mum!” she cried, dancing through the doorway. “Now can I join ballet school? Pretty please?”

Bella's mum sighed. “I'm really sorry, Bella. But we just can't afford the lessons.”

Bella trudged back to the charity shop.

“I'd like to return my leotard, tutu and slippers please,” she sighed.

“I'm sorry,” said the lady behind the counter. “We don't do refunds.”

“That's okay,” Bella shrugged. “You can

have them anyway. Sell them to someone who can afford ballet lessons. They make me too sad."

"I'm sorry," the lady said, shaking her head. "I can't take them back."

Bella looked up at her, confused.

"You might need them one day," the lady added, winking. "Don't give up on your dreams."

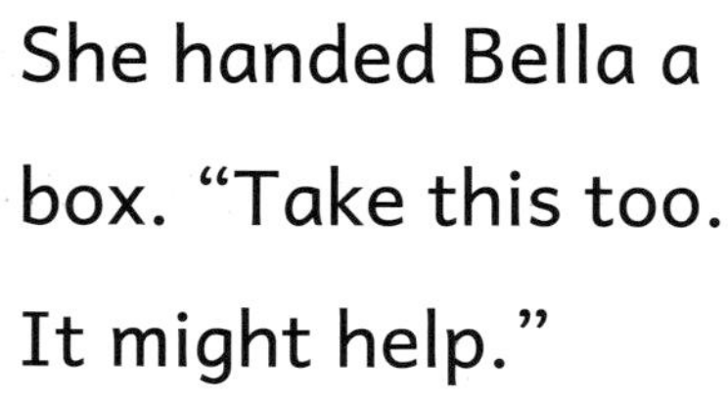

She handed Bella a box. "Take this too. It might help."

Bella opened the box. Inside, there was a tiny ballerina who twirled around as music played. But Bella didn't see how it could help.

"I don't have any money," Bella sighed.

"No need. It's a gift," the lady said, smiling. "Good luck, Bella."

"Thank you," Bella said. She didn't remember telling the lady her name.

Chapter 2

That night, Bella was just drifting off to sleep when the music-box started playing.

Bella opened her eyes. The box was glowing! She tiptoed over to the box and opened it slowly.

Inside, the tiny ballerina twirled around happily...

Then suddenly, she waved at Bella!

Bella gasped, then blinked. She must be dreaming. She pinched her arm to wake herself up.

“Ouch!” she yelped. She definitely wasn't asleep!

“Hello Bella!” the ballerina cried leaping out of her box. “My name's Marie! Lovely to meet you!”

“Um, lovely to meet you too,” Bella said, as Marie danced around her desk. “I wish I could dance like you.”

“Would you like me to teach you?” Marie offered.

“Yes please!” Bella cried. “That would be wonderful!”

Bella and Marie danced and danced, until Bella started to yawn.

“Bedtime,” Marie said, hopping back into her box. “See you tomorrow night. Sweet dreams!”

Bella smiled as she closed the lid. “Sweet dreams, Marie.”

Chapter 3

The next morning when Bella woke up, she opened her music-box eagerly. But the ballerina didn't wave or smile or talk. Bella sighed. Had it all just been a wonderful dream?

But that night, as the moon rose high in the sky, the music-box began to glow again. It was time for Bella's second ballet lesson!

Every evening from then on, Marie gave Bella ballet lessons. And with every lesson Bella got better and better.

Then one day Bella saw a poster for a talent competition.

"You should enter!" Marie cried when Bella told her about it. "The prize money would pay for ballet lessons!"

Bella bit her lip. "Do you really think I'm good enough?"

"If you practise really hard, definitely!" Marie said, beaming.

Bella practised VERY hard.

She practised while she brushed her teeth... while she made her breakfast... on the way to school and back again... she practised everywhere!

Finally the day of the talent contest arrived. Bella packed her ballet slippers, tutu, and

leotard. At the last minute she packed her music-box too.

She was very nervous.

"Relax," her mum smiled. "You love dancing more than anything. Just go out there and enjoy yourself."

Bella hugged her, then went to get changed.

Backstage, everyone was a bag of nerves. The clown got the giggles, the jugglers got the jitters, the singers got the hiccups.

Bella opened her music-box and stared at Marie.

"I can't believe you talked me into this," Bella hissed. "I've never been so nervous!"

Suddenly, someone tapped Bella on the shoulder, making her jump.

"You're up next," a guy said.

Chapter 4

The Mayor announced Bella's name and she stepped tentatively onto the stage. The lights were very hot and very bright. Bella felt her palms grow sweaty.

She couldn't do this. What was she thinking?

Then she spotted her mum in the front row, smiling at her. Suddenly the audience didn't seem so scary.

Then, as the music started, Bella forgot everything else. The music swept through Bella, carrying her away with it as she twirled and leaped and danced around the stage.

She forgot all about the contest and the prize and the audience, and danced just because she loved it so much.

When the music stopped the audience burst into applause. Bella beamed, bowed and hurried offstage to wait for the results.

“In third place,” the Mayor announced. “Colin the Clown!”

Everybody clapped. Bella swallowed hard.

This was more nerve-racking than dancing!

“In second place, Marvin the Magician!”

Everyone clapped again. Bella closed her eyes.

“Finally...” the Mayor paused. “In first place is...”

Bella crossed her fingers tightly.

“Sven the sword-swallower!”

Bella froze. She didn't win. She didn't get the prize money.

She would never go to ballet school.

Chapter 5

“Bella!” her mum called, running over to her afterwards. “Well done! You were wonderful!”

“Thanks,” Bella said sadly. “But I wasn't good enough.”

“It's not all about winning, love,” her mum said, hugging her. “There were so many different kinds of acts, it must've been difficult to judge. Did you have fun? That's the important thing!"

"Yes," Bella said, smiling as she remembered how the music had brought her to life - just like the music-box did with Marie. "It was the best moment of my life!"

"I could tell," a lady nearby commented. "You were the best dancer in the show by a mile."

"Thank you so much," Bella said, blushing.

"Which ballet school do you go to?" the lady asked.

“Oh, I don't,” Bella sighed.

“What?” the lady gasped. “Then my dear, you must join my ballet school!”

Bella blinked in surprise as the lady gave her a business card.

“It opened a few weeks ago, here in town. Please say you'll join?”

“I'd love to,” Bella sighed. “But ballet lessons are very expensive.”

“I won't take no for an answer,” the lady said. “My dear, you were born to dance. I'd like to offer you a full scholarship.”

Bella couldn't believe her ears. “Really? I could go to ballet school - for free?”

The lady smiled. “Is that a yes?”

Bella looked at her mum, who gave her a double thumbs up with a big smile.

“Yes!” Bella cried, leaping up and down.

"Wonderful!" the lady beamed. "I'll see you on Monday evenings at six."

"Thank you!" Bella cried as she walked away.

"Well done!" Bella's mum cried, hugging her. "That's fantastic!"

"Thanks," Bella beamed. She couldn't wait to tell Marie!

As Bella headed backstage she heard a familiar tune. She hurried inside to find a little boy dancing around in front of her

music-box. The boy froze when he saw Bella.

"I'm so sorry I opened your music-box," he said quickly. "But the music was so lovely and the little ballerina's so pretty and I just wanted to dance like you. I dream of becoming a ballet dancer one day!"

"It's okay," Bella said, smiling. "This is Marie. Thanks to her, I'm going to ballet school. I couldn't have done it without her."

Bella looked down at Marie, and swore she saw the tiny ballerina smile a little wider. Suddenly Bella had an idea.

"Why don't you keep the music-box?" she offered.

The little boy's eyes widened. "Really?"

Bella nodded, and grinned. "Marie just might help your dreams come true too."

The End

Pink
Red
Yellow
Blue
Green
Orange
Turquoise
Purple
Gold
White

The Institute of Education book banding system is a scale of colours that reflects the various levels of reading difficulty. The bands are assigned by taking into account the content, the language style, the layout and phonics. Word, phrase and sentence level work is also taken into consideration.

Maverick Early Readers are a bright, attractive range of books covering the pink to white bands. All of these books have been book banded for guided reading to the industry standard and edited by a leading educational consultant.

To view the whole Maverick Readers scheme, visit our website at
www.maverickearlyreaders.com

Or scan the QR code above to view our scheme instantly!